STAYING COOL

Nancy Antle ▪ pictures by E. B. Lewis

Dial Books for Young Readers **New York**

■ Author's Note ■

An amateur boxer must be at least seventeen years old
to compete at the national level of the Golden Gloves tournament.
However, cities all over the United States hold local Golden
Gloves tournaments and in these the minimum age requirement
varies. In St. Louis, where I observed the tournament, boys as
young as eight were allowed to participate.

Published by Dial Books for Young Readers
A Division of Penguin Books USA Inc.
375 Hudson Street • New York, New York 10014

Text copyright © 1997 by Nancy Antle
Pictures copyright © 1997 by E. B. Lewis
All rights reserved • Designed by Amelia Lau Carling
Printed in Hong Kong • First Edition
1 3 5 7 9 10 8 6 4 2

Library of Congress Cataloging in Publication Data
Antle, Nancy.
Staying cool/ by Nancy Antle; pictures by E. B. Lewis.—1st ed. p. cm.
Summary: While training in his grandfather's gym to compete
in the Golden Gloves amateur boxing tournament,
Curtis also has his eye on bigger prizes.
ISBN 0-8037-1876-4 (trade).—ISBN 0-8037-1877-2 (lib. bdg.)
[1. Boxing—Fiction. 2. Grandfathers—Fiction.] I. Lewis, Earl B., ill. II. Title.
PZ7.A6294St 1997 [E]—dc20 96-10992 CIP AC

The full-color artwork was prepared using watercolors.
It was then scanner-separated and reproduced as red, blue, yellow, and black halftones.
Gyms are very monochromatic, with the only colors being derived from the attire and
animation of the people. To reflect this, the artist has painted people in the backgrounds deliberately
in silhouette, and the main characters in the foregrounds in vibrant colors.

For Rick —N.A.

For Mr. Mitchell Allen
and all of the athletes at the Happy Hollow Gym —E.B.L.

"Hey, Curtis, how was school?" Grandpa asks. He grins his big grin at me.

"Fine," I say. I grin back at him. But I don't want to talk about school. I want to talk about boxing.

Every day after school I rush over to Grandpa's place. He has a gym in a boarded-up corner grocery store. Today I have lots of homework to do at Grandpa's big desk in the back. So boxing talk has to wait. I open my math book and start doing long-division problems.

Charles comes to put his bag in the locker next to the desk.

Charles is tall and has big muscles. He's a professional fighter—he boxes for money. Grandpa says Charles is one of the very best boxers he's ever trained. I hope I can box as well as Charles someday.

"You going to the Golden Gloves this year?" he asks me.

The Golden Gloves is an amateur boxing tournament. I want to be in it more than anything and make Grandpa proud. But I have to wait until Grandpa says okay.

"I hope I get to go," I say to Charles. "It's up to Grandpa. I've been training hard."

"You stay cool and don't lose your head, you'll be all right," Charles says. He goes off to do sit-ups.

I know what he means by "stay cool." Last week when I was sparring with my good friend Trevor, he hit me really hard in the stomach and it made me mad. I started hitting him like crazy. Then our feet got all tangled up and we both fell over. Grandpa said I lost control.

"Sparring is for learning," Grandpa said. "You didn't learn nothing from that. If you can't stay in control, you can't go to the Golden Gloves."

I know Grandpa was right, and it worries me. I hope Grandpa will let me spar again so that I can show him I can stay cool. At least I'll try. It's hard to stay cool when you get hurt.

Trevor hasn't been to the gym since that day. His sweaty old clothes are still in the same place he left them last week. Grandpa says he's seen him out running every morning, but I wish he'd come back so I can tell him I'll try to stay cool from now on.

I have a hard time doing my homework today because all I can think about is going to the Golden Gloves and winning and Grandpa hurting my eyes with his big grin.

On Grandpa's desk there is a picture of a young fighter hitting another fighter with a powerful left hook. That's Grandpa when he was a boxer. He was one of the best.

"I wanted to be Middleweight Champion of the World," he tells people. "But I never got a shot at the title." He sounds sad when he says it.

Now he's hoping that someday one of the guys he trains will get a title shot. I tell Grandpa it's going to be me. He just smiles and says, "One step at a time."

Usually I don't hear the noises in the gym when I'm doing my home-work. Today I hear them all. The noisiest thing is the timer. HONK! it goes off after every three minute workout period. HONK! again when the one minute rest period is over. During the three minute workout period I hear the rhythmic sound of the speed bag going *bumpitybumpity bumpity;* the dull THUD…THUDTHUD of the heavy bag being hit; the *whap whap whap* of jump ropes; and the snorts and heavy breathing of all the fighters working out. I start sweating just thinking about all that hard work.

Finally I finish my homework. I go to see what Grandpa wants me to do today.

"Curtis, get me those hand wraps," Grandpa says. Grandpa shows a new kid how to wrap his hands. Then the kid won't hurt them when he punches.

"Curtis, fill up the ice bag," Grandpa says a few minutes later. He puts the ice bag on a big man's shoulder. The man hurt it practicing his hook.

"Curtis, show Tony how to jump rope," Grandpa says next. Jumping rope is hard to learn. Tony's not much bigger than me and having lots of trouble.

"It took me a long time to learn too," I say to him. Tony smiles.

Men come to the gym after work to box. Kids come after school. Grandpa charges the men for using his gym, but the kids get to work out for free if they get good grades on their report cards.

Grandpa expects everyone who comes to his gym to work hard.

The regulars work out every day. There are always some new people too. They shadowbox. They hit the heavy bag, the speed bag, the double end bag. They lift weights. They do push-ups and sit-ups. They jump rope. They even stand on their head.

Early in the morning, when I'm still in bed, Grandpa does road work with some of them. They go on a three or four mile run—throwing punches at first, then just running—fast.

There are always fighters sparring at the gym every day too. I hope Grandpa will tell me to spar today. I start working out. I throw lots of punches and practice my footwork. Grandpa comes over and holds the punch mitts for me. He shows me where to put my feet so I keep my balance.

During a rest period Trevor walks in. He waves at me. He's not mad, I can tell. I'm glad.

"Curtis, get in the ring and spar with Trevor," Grandpa says after awhile. My stomach does a flip and I run over to the ring. Grandpa helps me and Trevor put on the big sparring gloves and headgear.

When the buzzer sounds, we start.

I hit Trevor with some good shots. He hits me too. The first couple hurt, but I keep telling myself to stay cool and think about throwing good punches and blocking Trevor's punches.

Grandpa paces around the outside of the ring yelling instructions.

"Get your hands up, Curtis!"

"Shoot that jab, Trevor!"

"Block that body shot, Curtis. He's getting you every time with it!"

"Jab, Trevor, jab!"

It's hard to listen and box at the same time.

Finally, at the end of the second round Grandpa says to quit. Trevor and I are both tired. It was hard, but I stayed cool. I am glad it's over.

"Good job," I say to Trevor.

"You too," he says.

"I think I have me two fighters ready for the Golden Gloves this year," Grandpa says.

"All right!" I say.

"Great!" Trevor yells. We give each other high fives. I hug Grandpa right there in front of everyone.

"You've both worked hard," Grandpa says. "Course, it don't hurt you none to have the best trainer in the business." He winks at me.

I climb out of the ring. I'm too happy to sit still for long. I pull a chair over to the speed bag and start punching it.

"Watch out," Charles teases. "Curtis is cookin'!"

One by one the fighters all go home or to work the night shift. Grandpa and I hang up hand wraps and put away gloves and headgear.

I lock up the gym for Grandpa. My stomach rumbles. Grandpa laughs.

"I think I smell your mama's corn bread," he says. "That'll fix you."

I laugh too, but I don't want to talk about corn bread. I want to talk about boxing.

"Grandpa, were you sorry you didn't get a chance to be Middleweight Champion?" I ask.

"I surely was," he says. "But now when one of the boxers from our gym fights and does his very best—I feel like a champion."

I smile. I like the way he says "our gym."

"Someday I'm going to fight for the Middleweight Championship just for you, Grandpa," I say.

"One step at a time," he says. "First you go to the Golden Gloves."

"I'm going to win that for you too," I say.

"You have to do it for yourself," Grandpa says.

"I'll do it for both of us," I say. "I'll make you proud."

"I'm already proud of you," Grandpa says, hurting my eyes with his big grin.

Then Grandpa and I go home to supper.